Surprise!

Surprise!

Written by Mary Packard
Illustrated by Benrei Huang

My First READER

SCHOLASTIC INC.

New York Toronto London Auckland Sydney
Mexico City New Delhi Hong Kong Buenos Aires

ISBN 0-516-24800-6

12 11 10 9 8 7 6 5 4 3 2 1 4 5 6 7 8 9/0

Printed in the U.S.A. 61

First Scholastic printing, April 2004

Note to Parents and Teachers

Once a reader can recognize and identify the 16 words used to tell this story, he or she will be able to read successfully the entire book. These 16 words are repeated throughout the story, so that young readers will be able to easily recognize the words and understand their meaning.

The 16 words used in this book are:

a	plane
ball	squeaks
doll	surprise
game	take
hides	toy
inside	train
it	what
peek	what's

A surprise!

What's inside?

A ball?

A game?

A plane?

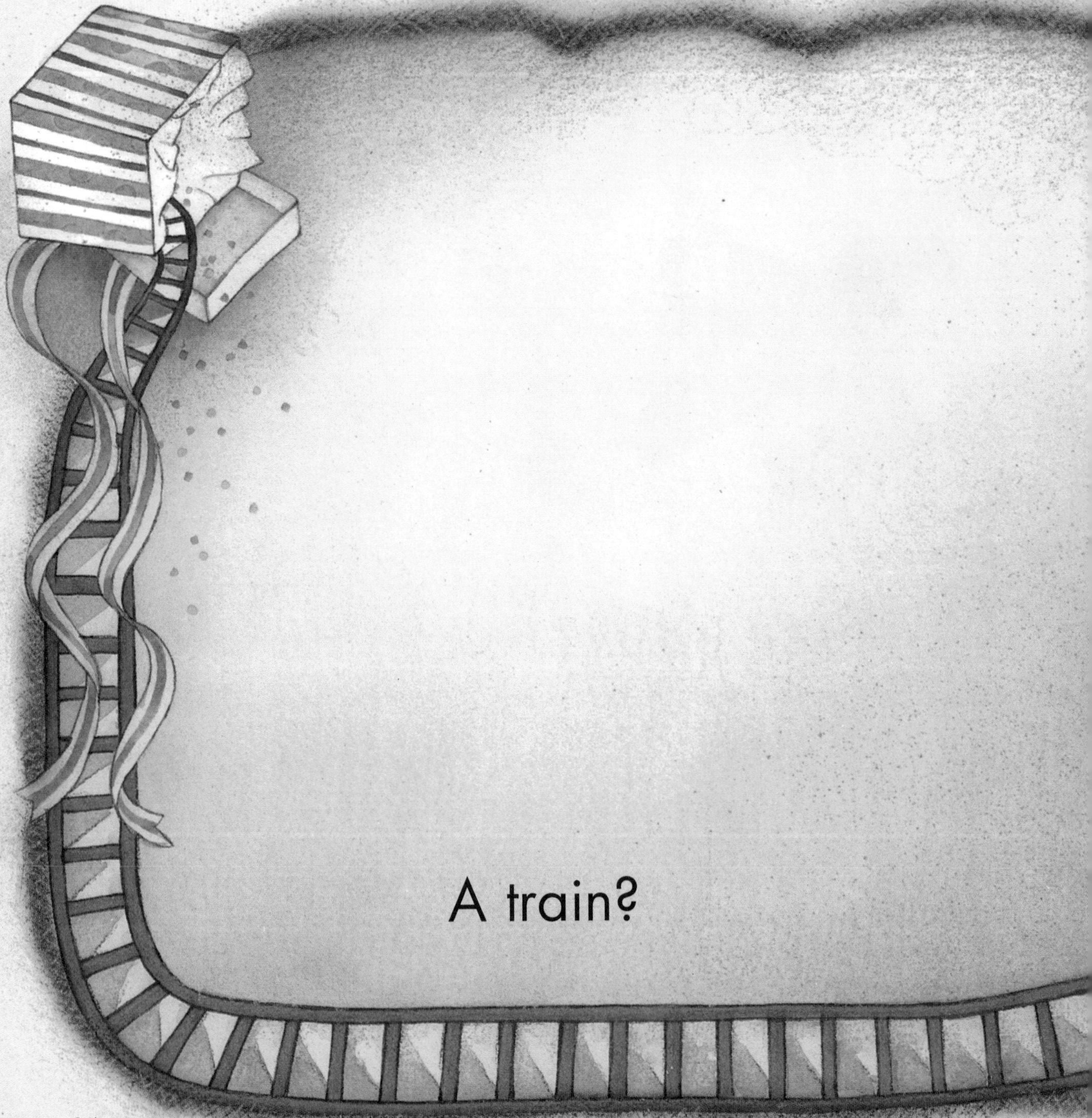

A train?

What hides inside?

It squeaks!

What squeaks inside?

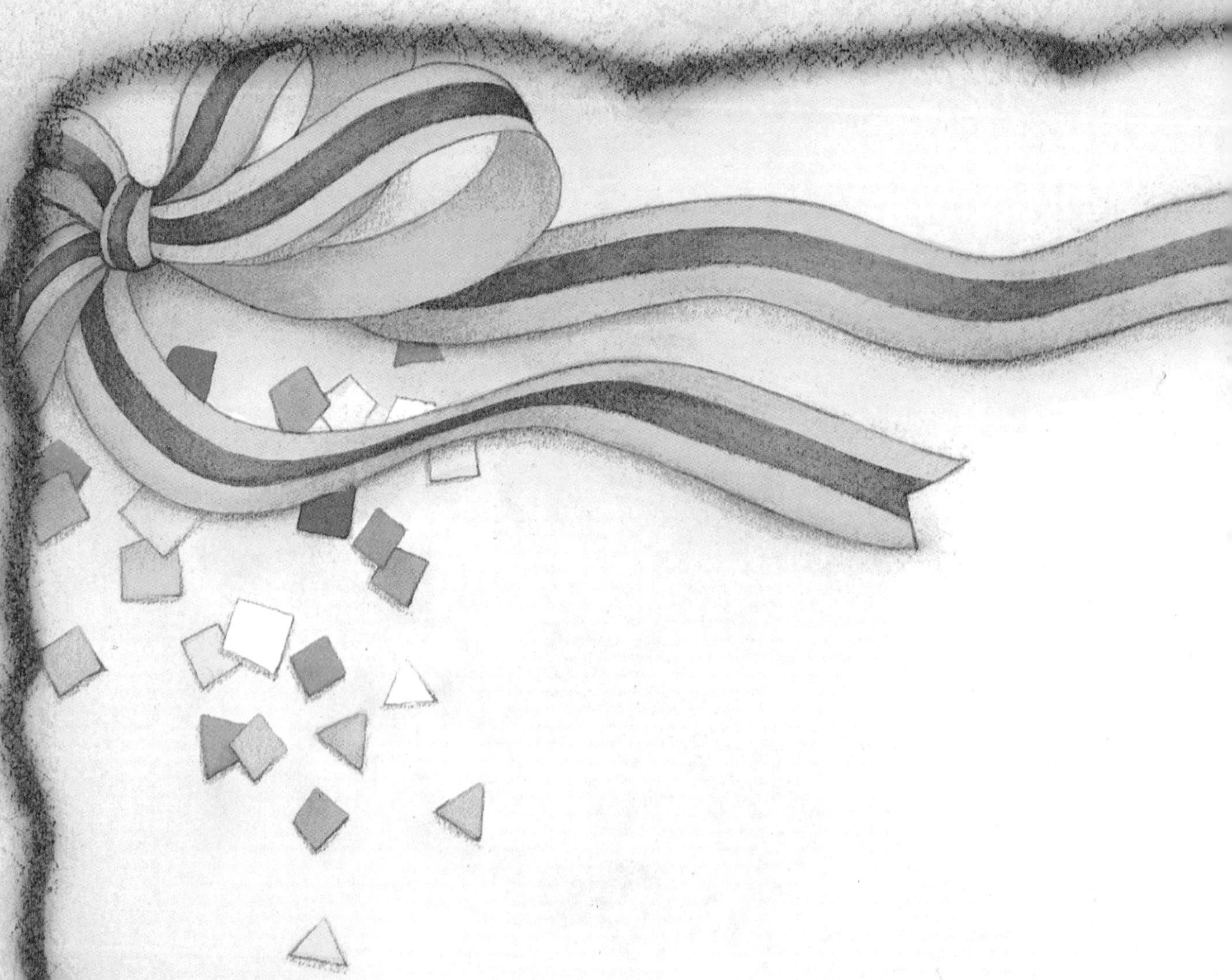

A doll?

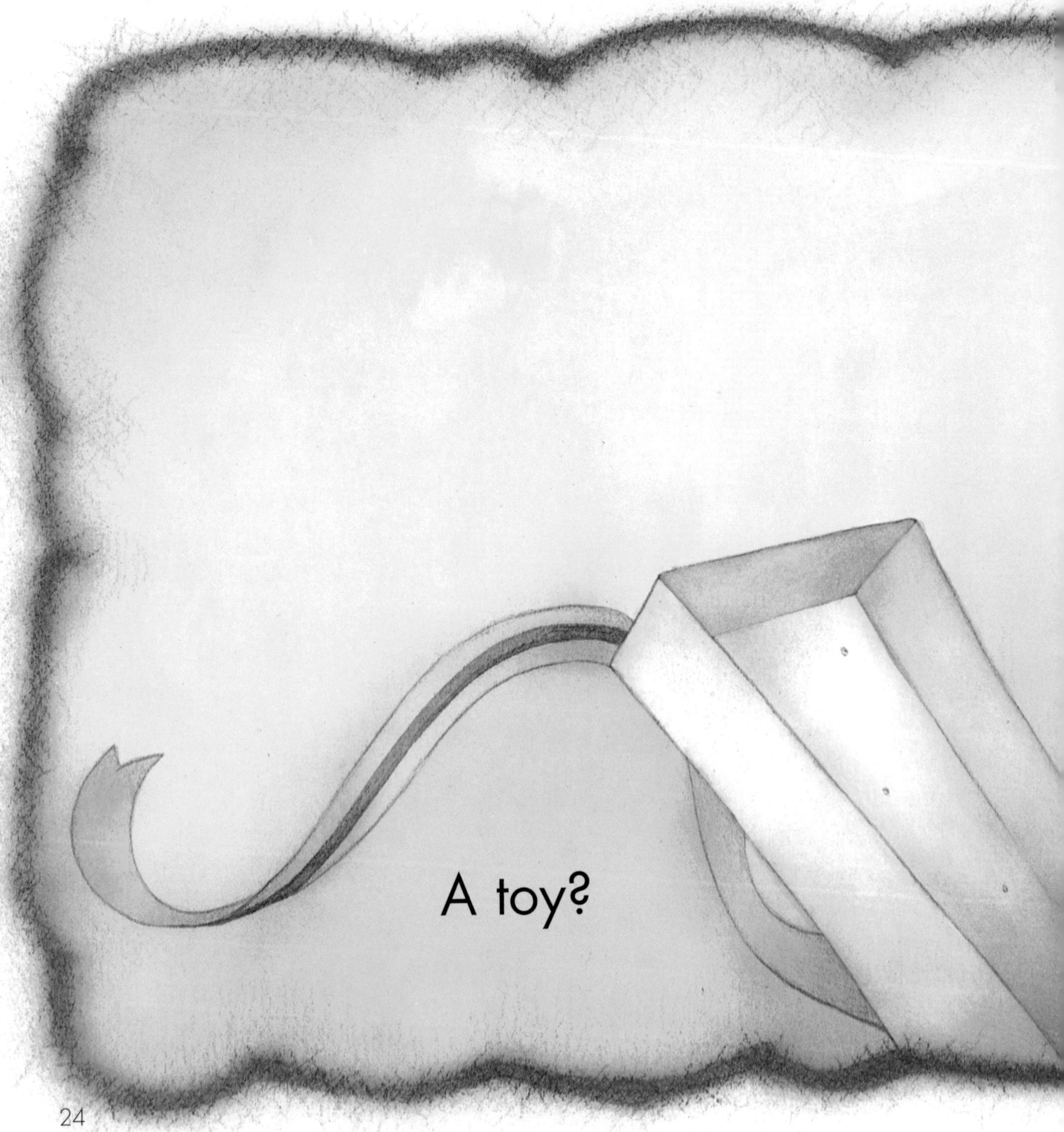

A toy?

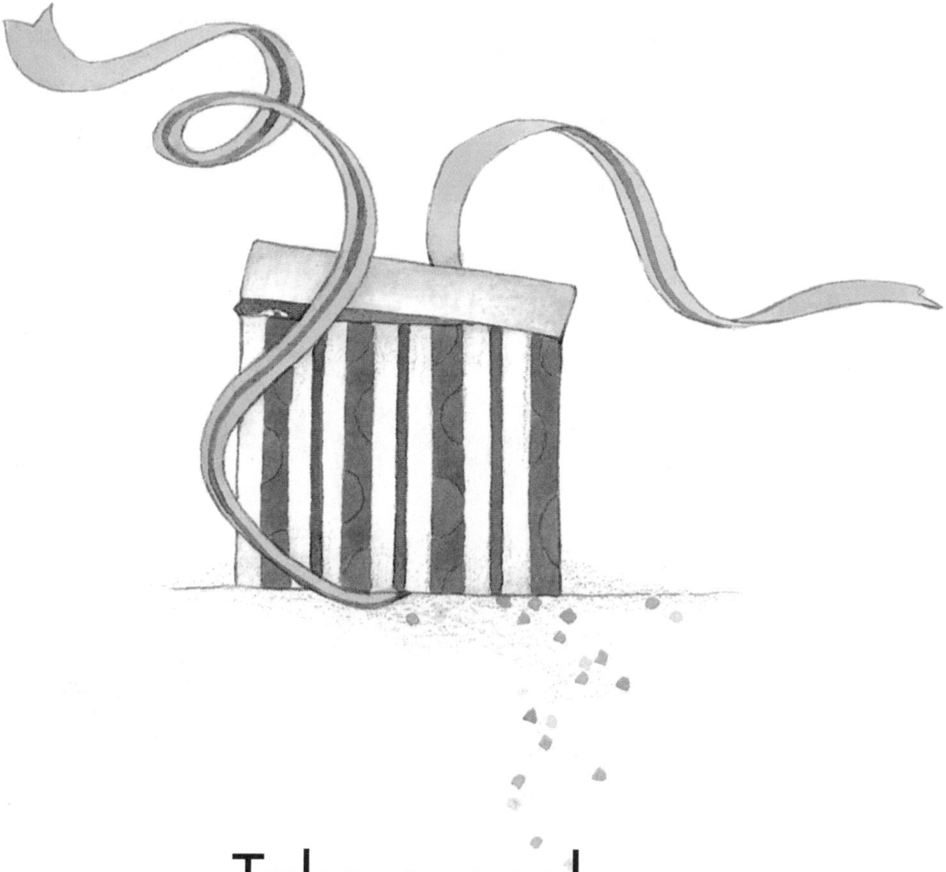

Take a peek.

Surprise!

ABOUT THE AUTHOR

Mary Packard has been writing children's books for as long as she can remember. Packard lives in Northport, New York, with her family. Besides writing, she loves music, theater, animals, and, of course, children of all ages.

ABOUT THE ILLUSTRATOR

Benrei Huang received her master's in illustration from the School of Visual Arts. She has illustrated more than thirty children's books. Huang lives in New York City with her husband and young son.